Reindeer on the Roof.com

Created by: Michael Bovill

Illustrated by
Jeff Roux and Ben Sawyer

Co-Written:
Alexandra Bovill & Kimberly Parente

Book designed by: Imaginary Kidz

Created by: Michael Bovill

Illustrations provided by Brave River Solutions

Editing by Beth Googins

Co Writers: Alexandra Bovill & Kimberly Parente

For general information on our other products call 401-301-3976 or
www.imaginarykidz.com

ISBN 978-0-9852292-1-4

Printed in the People's Republic of China

Cast of Characters

Holly

Nicholas

Santa

Wimbley

Reindeer on the Roof

Tracker

One frosty morning in early November, the sun was trying to peek through the milky white sky while tiny snowflakes gently fluttered in the air. Not even noticing the cold, Wimbley, Santa's right-hand elf, skipped merrily up the path to Santa's house. When he rang the doorbell he could hear Tracker, Santa's puppy, scurrying to the door to greet him. Mrs. Claus barely had the door open before Tracker jumped at Wimbley, knocking him down and licking his face with his wet, slobbery tongue.

"Hee, hee, hee," laughed Wimbley as Mrs. Claus helped him to his feet. Mrs. Claus seemed especially happy to see Wimbley this morning. "Thank goodness you are here. I really think Santa could use your help. He seems unusually flustered this morning," she said.

"No worries," Wimbley replied. "Tracker and I always seem to brighten his day." Wimbley then skipped down the hall with Tracker following at his heels. The office door was shut so Wimbley jumped onto Tracker's back so that he could reach the door knob. As he opened the door, he was surprised to find Santa sitting at his desk with his head in his hands. This was very puzzling, because ordinarily Santa was very holly jolly, especially in the morning.

"Santa, what on earth is wrong?" Wimbley asked. Wimbley noticed that Santa's face was pale and he looked worried.

"We have a big problem!" Santa exclaimed. "Our post office is too small and can't handle all the letters that the children are sending. I am afraid I might not be able to receive all the children's Christmas lists this year!" He slid back into his velvety red chair and sighed. "We need to fix this problem quickly; we need a plan!"

Wimbley hopped up onto the couch to think. Tracker plopped himself down on the floor right beneath Wimbley's feet, and let out a long sigh of his own.

A little while later, Mrs. Claus came in with a tray of muffins and two mugs of steaming hot cocoa. "I figured you could use some breakfast to help you think," she said.

Wimbley bit into a warm chocolate chip muffin. "You know these help me think the best," Wimbley said as he wiped some chocolate from his mouth.

"That's what I'm counting on Wimbley!" Mrs. Claus said as she gently closed the door.

A few moments later, Wimbley jumped down from the couch, hopped over Tracker, and began to pace back and forth in front of Santa's desk.

"I think I've got it!" Wimbley exclaimed. "Before I came over here this morning, I was out making my rounds. As you are aware, we had an unusually high number of miniature reindeer born last spring. In fact, the elves over at the barn are having a hard time caring for all of these adorable babies. Maybe we can choose some of the most responsible and well-behaved children in the world to help us care for these newborn reindeer for a little while."

"Umm, excuse me Wimbley. I'm sorry to interrupt." Santa chimed in, "but maybe the hot cocoa went to my head. How, exactly, will this help us with the letter problem?"

"Don't you see?" Wimbley responded. "That is the beauty of my idea. The children will be helping us care for the reindeer, and the reindeer will help us by delivering the Christmas lists to us while the children are sleeping. Don't worry Santa, I'll explain it all to you over lunch. Let's go see what Mrs. Claus is cooking. It smells delicious and I haven't eaten in minutes."

Over a scrumptious lunch of peanut butter, banana, and chocolate chip sandwiches, Wimbley filled Santa in on the details of his plan. Once he was finished, hope began to flicker in Santa's heart.

"Wimbley, you have outdone yourself once again. Your plan is brilliant and I know just the children that we can use to test it out! Let's get a package ready for the Huxley family home. There are two very special children who live there." With those words Santa lifted Wimbley onto his shoulders and they scrambled out to the barn with Tracker bounding close behind them. They were all very eager to put together the very special package that would be delivered that night to Holly and Nicholas Huxley.

The next morning, Holly Huxley woke to find a package on the table beside her bed. "Mom, Dad, come quickly," cried Holly. "I have a present from Santa with a note attached to it!"

"Me too, me too!" Nicholas shouted from across the hall.

"Come to Holly's room and let's see what you have," called Mom and Dad.

The whole family met in Holly's room and Holly began reading the note that was attached to her gift.

"Dear Holly,
I really need your help this Christmas season. Inside this package is one of my newborn miniature reindeer and a special barn for him. We are so busy here at the North Pole getting ready for Christmas that we can't give this little guy all of the love and attention that he deserves. Please give him your love. Also, when you have it written, please place your Christmas list in the reindeer's saddlebag. Then, put the reindeer on the roof of the barn. This magical reindeer will fly to me and give me your Christmas list and any wishes you would like to share with me.

"My letter says the same thing!" exclaimed Nicholas.

"Oh, that is so special!" exclaimed Mom. "Santa must have known that the two of you are very responsible and caring. I told you that Santa is always watching!"

"He sure is!" agreed Nicholas. "We are going to take great care of our little reindeer!".

..and we are going to be on our best behavior!" added Holly.

Well, what a day it turned out to be! Holly and Nicholas couldn't stop playing with their new reindeer.

"What are you going to name your reindeer?" asked Mom.

"I think I am going to call mine Snowball, because it reminds me of the North Pole where Santa lives," replied Holly.

"I think I'm going to call my reindeer Snowflake because it reminds me of Christmas," said Nicholas.

"Well, I think that they are wonderful names," said Mom.

Soon it was time for Holly and Nicholas to go to bed. They both went to Holly's room to talk to their reindeer together.

"We love you Snowball and Snowflake. Will you please fly to the North Pole tonight with our Christmas lists and wishes and tell Santa that we have a special wish this year? What we would like for Christmas this year, more than any doll or any toy, is that our family and the families of all our friends will all be safe and warm and happy."

"Now we will put our letters in your saddlebags and place each of you on the roof of your barn," said Nick.

"How will we know that they flew back to the North Pole while we were sleeping?" Holly asked.

"The letter said that we will know that they flew to the North Pole if they are back inside their barns when we wake up tomorrow morning," answered Nicholas.

Nicholas said goodnight to Holly and went to his room with his reindeer and barn. The children had a little trouble falling asleep at first, but they were so tired from playing with Snowball and Snowflake all day that they soon nodded off.

CRASH!

Once they heard the gentle breathing of the children that signaled that they were fast asleep, Snowball and Snowflake used their magical hooves to take off into the night air. Up, up and away they flew. Just a few moments later, Snowball and Snowflake's antlers could be heard crashing into Santa's door.

Santa opened the door and lying right in front of him were Snowball and Snowflake.

"Well, well, hello Snowball and Snowflake. Please come in and get warm by the fire," invited Santa.

Snowball and Snowflake came in and talked happily about Holly and Nicholas and how much they really loved their new home. They gave Santa the children's Christmas lists and wishes.

"Well thank you for helping me by coming and giving me Nicholas and Holly's lists," Santa said. "I know you are in loving hands at their house and I am sure that you are eager to get back. I'll see you very soon."

Off went Snowball and Snowflake back to Nicholas and Holly's bedrooms where they snuggled down inside their barns.

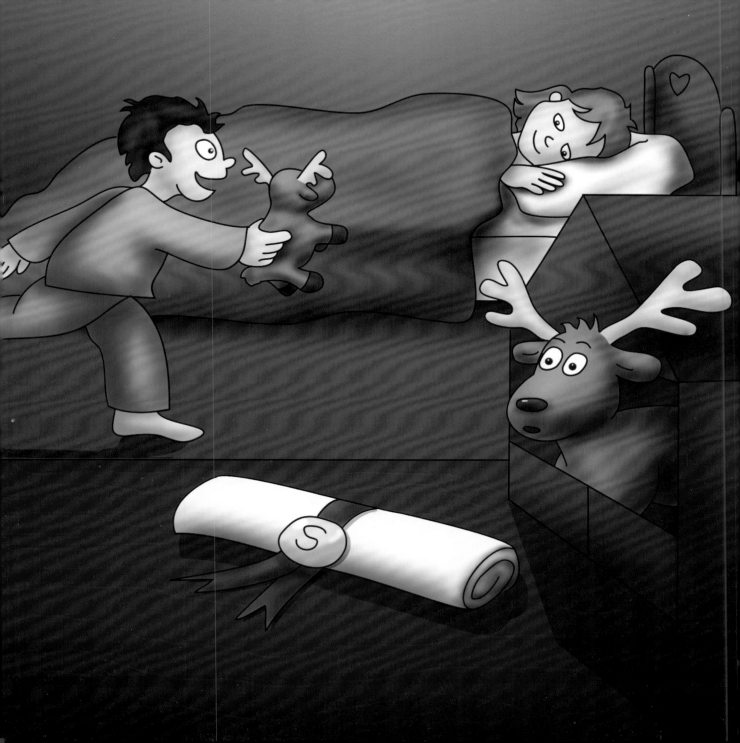

The next morning when their alarm clocks sounded, Nicholas and Holly's eyes flew open. They quickly glanced at their reindeer barns and saw that their reindeer were back inside! Nicholas jumped up first and came running into Holly's room with his reindeer.

They both called out in really loud voices, "Mommy, Daddy, come quickly!!!"

As Mom and Dad came running in, Nicholas exclaimed, "Snowball and Snowflake are back in their barns. We put them on the roofs of the barns last night so that means they flew to the North Pole and gave Santa our letters!"

"..and I found a letter next to my barn," added Holly. "It is addressed to both of us!"

"This is so wonderful, you now have a special way to talk to Santa," replied Dad.

"Please read Santa's letter for us," Mom requested.

"Okay," said the children. And Holly began to read for both of them.

Dear Holly and Nicholas,
I can see that you have been wonderful children this year and I want you to know that you are both at the very top of my NICE list. Wonderful job! I met your new reindeer, Snowball and Snowflake, last night and they said so many good things about you. They told me about your special Christmas wish and I am so proud to see that you understand the true meaning of Christmas. I knew that you were very special children and that is why I chose you to test out my new way to learn about the Christmas wishes of good boys and girls. Don't be surprised if you hear that some of your friends are soon asked to care for reindeer of their own. Thanks to you, my miniature reindeer, and the great idea of my right hand elf Wimbley, Christmas is saved!

I will see you on Christmas Eve!

Your Friend, Santa"

Holly and Nicholas were so excited about Santa's letter. Without even realizing it, they had become Santa's helpers. They continued to love and care for Snowball and Snowflake, and Holly even started calling Snowball her "Reindeer on the Roof", so that she would never forget the magical things he could do.

Reindeer on the Roof

Directions

Step 1

Write out your Christmas List

Step 2

Roll up your Christmas List and place it into your Reindeer's saddlebag

" Communicate with Santa through your Reindeer on the Roof. Send your Christmas List or Note directly to Santa."

Step 3

Place your Reindeer on the Roof

Step 4

When you fall asleep your Reindeer will fly to the North Pole and deliver your Christmas List to Santa

Sometimes Santa writes back!!

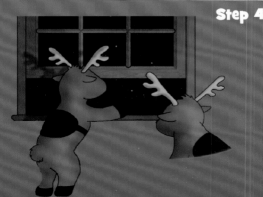